Escape from the Medieval Age

Steve Hurley

BEWARE:
*This is **not** a normal book!*

Within these pages are multiple adventures which you will have while trying to escape from the medieval age.

As you read through this book you will be faced with many decisions.

You must be careful.

If you choose well, you may manage to escape from the medieval age and return to the present…

but

…taking the wrong path could lead to your ultimate destruction or worse.

Have you got what it takes to succeed?

Now, turn to page 1.

Good Luck!

For the last few months you have been working on a secret project with a team of scientists from all over the world. You were especially chosen from among all the students in your country and have been training hard every day after college in a hidden underground laboratory.

This morning you are carrying out the final experiment. Utilising the delicate nature of quantum physics, you have finally discovered how to travel through time.

You personally volunteer to be the first to try the new machine. You are going to be sent back to the year 1347 – the medieval age!

You fidget nervously watching the technicians make the final adjustments to the machine. You remember from your history training that two kings were fighting for the throne at the time so you'll have to have all your wits about you to survive this romantic but violent time.

Turn to page 2.

2

A team of white-coated men and women are stood all around you, watching expectantly. The head scientist gives you a tiny circular device with a single button. It's about the size of a large coin.

"You'll need this to return," he says. "Just press the button when you are inside the machine and it will automatically return you to the present. You'll be returned to your most familiar surroundings and you will think everything is just a dream."

You take a step towards the machine.

It looks like a giant spring, pulsing up and down. It has an opening in one side and as it slowly grows in height, the opening becomes big enough for you to step into.

The machine flashes with a vivid turquoise-blue light, the brightness increasing as you step inside. You hear one of the scientists shout, "Ready... *now.*" A dull humming noise fills your ears, growing louder and louder until it is deafening. The blue lights flash faster. Then, you seem to go blind for a second as everything turns white. Trusting the scientists but feeling absolutely terrified, you squeeze your eyes shut, then... silence.

Turn to page 3.

You slowly open your eyes to find that you are surrounded by trees – massive trees. You would need four or five people just to hold hands around the trunk of one of these giants.

There is something else unnerving.

You stand on a muddy path for a while trying to figure out what it is, then it dawns on you. There's no noise. No traffic, no aeroplanes, nothing; only silence and the occasional bird singing in the treetops.

The machine behind you starts to hum again then in seconds it flashes and disappears. What? Where did it go?

Turn to page 4.

4

Back in the laboratory you had heard the scientists discussing the probability of a 'location jump' due to some minor technical errors with the machine. You check your pocket for the return device. Good, still there. The machine can't have gone far. All you have to do is survive long enough to track it down and return to your own time. You hope this will be as easy as it sounds.

You are dressed in a colourful medieval outfit and have only a few authentic medieval pennies which the scientists provided you with. You look around, taking in your unfamiliar surroundings. You are standing on a small hill at the edge of an enormous medieval forest. The muddy path you are standing on goes two ways. At the bottom of the hill you see a small medieval town.

If you head down to the town, turn to page 57.

If you decide to explore the forest, turn to page 9.

After your lucky escape from the soldiers the adrenaline is pumping through your body and the last thing you feel like doing is going back to sleep or hiding in a grimy pile of straw. You creep towards the shadowy trees of the ancient medieval forest.

It is hard going trying to pick your way between the dense trees in the black of night. A wolf howls every few minutes causing you to freeze, rooted to the spot, trying to guess how far away it is. You stumble a couple of times, and after a few hours, when the morning shades of red and yellow are beginning to show in the sky, you see bloody scratches on your arms and legs.

Your whole body aches from the night's exertion and the morning sunlight now allows you to forage for food for your grumbling stomach. You try a small red berry from a nearby bush but immediately spit it out – it tastes like sour milk! You see a rabbit darting across the path but you have no idea how you would cook it even if you could catch it.

You also realise that you wouldn't remember your way back to the town if you needed to turn back, and staring around at the never-ending trees, you feel a seed of panic take root.

Turn to page 14.

6

The first thing you notice as you enter the great hall is a gigantic roaring fire warming the whole room. You could park three or four cars inside that fireplace and the chimney must be enormous.

In front of you is a massive rectangular wooden table. It is covered with fine silver chalices and the food looks so beautiful you're not sure if it's edible or only for decoration. Dogs scamper around under the tables begging for scraps.

"I say, come hither valiant one," comes a shout from the head table. "Where have you been?"

It's Sir Donald, and he's seen you. He beckons for you to sit down next to him.

"May I have the pleasure of introducing His Majesty King Edward?"

Turn to page 88.

You move through the hustle and bustle to another part of the fair, near the town buildings. Looking over your shoulder you notice that the man with the cloak is still following you. He must have been watching you from afar during the bear baiting. Your heart beats faster as you walk on. Safer to try and blend in with the crowd – maybe he'll leave you alone then.

You pass a crackling hog turning slowly on a spit and a chubby woman sitting behind an assortment of pastries labelled 'Margy's Pies'. You hand Margy a few pennies and she passes you a steaming round pie.

"Wild rabbit love, trapped 'em meself I did," she beams cheerfully. You take a bite. Certainly tastes good. As you walk away you feel a hand clamp down on your shoulder.

"Say nothing, come with me," growls a voice in your ear. You spin around to see the cloaked man who has been following you. His hand is still on your shoulder squeezing tightly. "You're not safe here, come... NOW!" he hisses.

If you believe him and think it's best to do what he says, turn to page 86.

If you don't trust this stranger and want to make a run for it, turn to page 64.

8

The girl coughs again and snivels into the blanket which was once white. She looks sick and in need of a good meal. "Let's take her with us," you say, still trying to pull your arm from Sir Donald's vice-like grip.

"You do not understand." Sir Donald's face is solemn, the very picture of seriousness. "We *must* leave her. Get back on the horse. Heed my words."

You are surprised to see that Sir Donald looks almost... scared.

Well, you were brought up to help people when they are in trouble; especially a little defenceless girl!

If you pull away from Sir Donald and insist on helping the girl, turn to page 22.

If you 'heed' Sir Donald's words and leave the girl where she is, turn to page 109.

You still feel a bit disorientated and don't really want to be among strangers, especially medieval strangers. You turn towards the forest and start walking.

You've been in many forests before, near your home town, but never anything like this – it's enormous. You have the feeling you could journey for days and days and never see another soul, let alone cars, telegraph poles, old coke cans and other modern invaders.

Here, now, the trees are in command.

You arrived here very early in the morning and as you walk on, the blood-red sun begins to rise high into the sky, throwing shafts of sunlight into the shadows created by the surrounding trees. You stop next to a babbling brook and cup your hands to take a drink. The cool water tastes fresh and you decide this would be a good place to rest for a while. You sit with your aching feet in the water, a damp mossy smell filling your nostrils, and the spooky calls of the forest animals echoing all around you.

A few hours later you push yourself up from the riverbank and continue your journey, now deep in the forest.

Turn to page 28.

You smile to yourself. This riddle is so easy.

"The answer is ten," you state proudly. You are surprised when both the guards shake their heads in unison.

"You are wrong," says the tall guard, scratching under his helmet and looking bored. "The answer is higher than ten." The crossed spears stay crossed and you realise that there's no way you are going to enter the castle keep unless you can guess the answer to the riddle.

You can hear many voices now, coming from within. Everybody must be taking their places in the great hall for the feast. Sir Donald is waiting for you.

You must get past these troublesome guards!

Turn to page 136.

"I've got it!" you shout, a wide grin spreading across your face. "The answer is eleven." The guards look at each other and sigh audibly.

"We thought you had it for a moment. Close but not close enough." The spears stay crossed barring your way in. The shorter guard stares at the ground with bored, hooded eyes and lazily begins to pick his nose.

From inside the keep you can hear the sounds of people at work and the smell of roasting meat wafts out of a tiny slit window, causing your mouth to fill with saliva. You clench your fists in frustration. There's no way on earth you are getting inside unless you find the answer to the riddle.

Think, you tell yourself... *think!*

Turn to page 136.

12

You don't really want to waste the last few pennies you have on some crazy medieval medicine that may not even work.

"No thank you," you say. "It's probably just a bad cold. I'll be fine in a day or two."

A hand with a whip pokes out from behind the curtain, whips the mule into action and the wagon rattles away down the forest path.

"Time waster!" comes an angry yell as the wagon disappears from view.

What a rude man, you think to yourself. And why did he hide and tell me to leave the money on the grass?

Turn to page 121.

After telling you to relax and carefully washing your injured head, the monk introduces himself as Brother Hector – a Franciscan monk. You get dressed and he leads you down some stairs to a grand refectory where the other monks are eating. You sit and gape at the food-laden table. At last you can eat!

You shovel food into your mouth staring about the room. High stone walls decorated with beautiful coloured saints surround you. There are around twenty other monks whispering to each other at the table all dressed in the same brown robe. An ancient bent old man who seems to be in charge approaches you.

"Welcome to our humble abode," he smiles. "I am the abbot. I see young Brother Hector, our new resident doctor, has returned you to good health. He has only been with us for six months but already his powers of healing are second to none."

During the meal you answer the many questions the abbot has for you. You tell the monks about the wild boar and how you hit your head. When they ask where you are from, you pretend that you are from a neighbouring village. Brother Hector looks up from his plate and shoots you a strange look then pushes back his chair and leaves the table.

Turn to page 71.

14

As the sun reaches its zenith high above the forest, you feel hungrier than ever. How can you walk further on an empty stomach? Then, listening carefully, you can distinctly hear someone singing. You step around a giant oak tree and come to a clearing. Immediately you see the source of the forlorn melody.

An old woman is sat before you on a tree stump singing softly to herself. There is no one else to be seen. She stops and looks at you curiously. Her face is covered in a network of fine wrinkles and an enormous hairy wart protrudes from her nose. She reminds you of a fairy-tale witch but smells much worse.

"Come closer child," she beckons with a skeletal finger. You step closer but the smell forces you to keep your distance. "Don't be scared," she smiles, coughing into a handkerchief. "I am old and frail and have not known the joy of a kiss for many a year. I can help you but first you must kiss me." Still smiling she turns her cheek towards you expectantly.

If you brave the smell and the warts and kiss her, turn to page 77.

If you're not going anywhere near this hag, turn to page 90.

Henry rises to his feet and puts his arm around you, still trying to hold his mirth in. "Behold, our new court jester," proclaims Henry. The men all cheer in unison.

You realise that you are going to be spending a lot of time with these men now, whether you like it or not. You never thought of yourself as a comedian but as you gaze upon the grinning faces of the men you feel strangely proud. *Yes, why not? A jester's life is the life for me,* you think to yourself merrily.

You spend many years with Henry's gang living in the forest and keeping the men happy while they battle King Edward and his armies. As you grow older you forget all about the modern world. Television, cars, the Internet and school seem only distant dreams. You travel the land, making people laugh and forget their troubles wherever you go.

You live well and have many children who you hope will carry on the family tradition of laughter!

The End

Sir Donald kisses the lady upon her hand, leaving her blushing as he gallops off through the trees.

On your journey to the castle you learn that this 'lady' is actually a princess. She is the eldest daughter of King Edward, 'the good king'. You and Sir Donald have just prevented the robbery of the royal treasury, the entire wealth of the kingdom!

That evening in the great hall of the castle you are knighted personally by King Edward. You rise from your knees to great applause, a true knight of the realm.

Before long you forget all about the time machine and the twenty-first century. Within a year the land is gripped by a terrible plague but you survive, helping wherever you can. When the pestilence finally passes, you employ a squire and get down to the gritty business of protecting the innocent and punishing the wicked. The years go by...

A group of peasants are saved from a burning church... an assassination attempt on King Edward is thwarted... the forest roads are once again made safe to travel, all due to the exploits of the mysterious unknown knight with the unusual accent, known only as 'The Stranger'.

The End

You pull the front door closed behind you and leap onto the horse behind Sir Donald. As you leave the town you spin round in the saddle and watch the townsfolk packing away their stalls, clearing away the refuse after yesterday's fair.

The horse keeps to a leisurely walk but it's not long before you are completely surrounded by trees. It's darker and the air feels cooler beneath the boughs of the great oaks and bushy elm trees.

You notice that Sir Donald keeps his hand on the hilt of his sword. He catches your glance. "It pays well to be prepared whilst so deep in the forest," he says. "It is so easy for evil-doers to hide at will." You look around imagining eyes staring back at you from the shadows of the trees. You start to feel uncomfortable. Coming round the next bend in the path you forget all about your paranoia.

Before you, sat at the side of the path, is a small child huddled in a filthy blanket. It's a girl. She can't be more than eight years old.

Coughing into her blanket, she looks up at you both with tearful eyes.

Turn to page 105.

Just because someone tells you to do something, it doesn't mean you have to do it. You don't like the look of this man so you decide to make a run for it.

You pull away from him and run like hell. Back past the food stalls and around a copse of oak trees. Then you double back on yourself and creep into the deserted alleyways of the village.

Leaning on an old wooden barrel, you wipe the sweat from your forehead. *Phew, lost him!* It is then that you realise you're not the only one here in the empty streets. A small, shadowy, rat-faced figure appears in front of you. Then another two men approach from your left. They look poor and hungry – poor and dangerous.

You see the flash of steel as the first man takes a knife from his belt. All three of them are now stepping slowly towards you.

You are too busy with your eyes glued to the men in front of you to notice a fourth man creeping up behind the wooden barrel that you're leaning on. Too late you spin around, just in time to see a dirty knife plunge into your chest.

The End

A jug of ice cold water splashes across your face. It's the morning! Oopsy... you've spent the whole night snoring on the floor.

You lift your head and wince painfully as the morning sunlight beams into your eyes. Now you decide you *do* believe the Devil exists because he's living in your poor aching head!

You reach into your pocket and to your horror realise that the coin-sized return device is gone! Your night of drunkenness has cost you your only means of returning to the present.

You will have to live out the rest of your life here in the medieval times.

Hmm... maybe that's not so bad!

The End

20

You take a step back and lean against the grey stone wall thinking. After what seems like forever, you suddenly jump into the air... Eureka! The logical answer seemed like it should be ten or eleven, but then again, since when has a riddle been logical?

Of course, when you think about it, the man must paint the number '9' twenty times in total. This is because when he reaches the number '90', all of the following numbers have a '9' at the beginning: 91, 92, 93…etc. And '99' has two. Add these to the nines at the end of the numbers and you reach twenty 'nines' in total. Got it?

The guards both pat you on the back. "Well done, you are not as stupid as you look." They smile, again mocking your badly chosen medieval attire. They stand aside and allow you to pass under the thick stone archway and into the main keep.

The murmuring of voices echoes down the passage. The feast has begun. Following the voices and even more the smells, you finally pass through a massive, heavy, royal red curtain and into the great hall.

Turn to page 6.

All that walking has made you thirsty, so you decide to brave the medieval inn and sample the local brew. You push the wooden door open and go in.

A large fire in the centre of the room bellows out smoke, only some of which escapes through the small chimney hole in the roof. A buxom bar wench skilfully manoeuvres between the various wooden tables, balancing a tray of drinks on her arm. You notice something curious – no-one is smoking. Of course, tobacco hasn't been discovered yet, but it's smoky enough without it!

You decide to take a small table in a corner. After a minute or so, a short, fat, ruddy-faced man wearing a filthy apron comes over and offers his hand.

"Innkeeper Barnaby at your service," he pumps your hand enthusiastically. "Will you be requiring a room for the night?" You reply that you won't and ask for a flagon of ale. "Very good. Here at the Gnarly Goat we serve the best ale in the county," he says, before returning to the kitchen.

He seems a friendly type, you think to yourself. It must be your strange clothes. Maybe he thinks you're wealthy or important! A moment later the bar wench slams a frothing flagon of ale down on your table.

Turn to page 23.

22

You yank your arm out of Sir Donald's grip and cross the path towards the little girl. The horse begins to whinny nervously.

"If you take one more step I'm going to have to leave you here," calls Sir Donald, turning the skittish horse around ready to go.

"OK then," you spit. "Abandon me *brave* knight."

Sir Donald shakes his head sadly and whips his horse into a gallop, disappearing down the muddy path.

Turn to page 117.

You gulp down your ale thirstily, taking in the atmosphere. The floor and tables are sticky with old beer and you notice quite a few customers curled up in their cloaks asleep. You remember reading that sleeping on the floor downstairs, as well as in the rooms upstairs, was commonplace in medieval inns.

You are distracted from your thoughts by loud shouts coming from the other side of the room. You see two men arguing.

"I'm no liar Leofric. I *did* see a blue flash in the forest this morning," whines a short, pale man with grey, lank hair.

"Heresy! You say an angelic light came to you, Gwynn? You could hang for such talk." The larger, bearded man, Leofric, puts his hand on the hilt of his sword.

"I don't know what made the flash you big hairy fool, but I saw it," replies the smaller Gwynn.

A flash in the forest? Could it be that this man saw you arrive in the machine this morning?

If you walk up to the arguing men and politely ask what exactly Gwynn saw and if he knows more, turn to page 91.

If you decide to stay put and order another flagon of ale, turn to page 51.

How can one win against four no matter how big the bear is? You bet on the dogs. The bearded man with the scars barks 'fight' and cuts the chain.

The first dog jumps straight at the bear but, before its muzzle even gets within biting distance, the bear whacks it out of the way with the swipe of a huge paw, opening its belly all over the grass. The next two dogs jump together. One of them, a skinny black dog with one ear, gets a grip on the bear's flank. It holds on for a few seconds then the bear rolls onto its side and crushes both dogs instantly. You wince at the sickening crunching sound.

Now the last dog – a big brute of a dog; it is orange and black with teeth like a shark! It growls deep in the back of its throat and jumps. The bear is caught around the neck by the dog's massive jaws. After a few tense seconds of flailing around, the bear falls forward but the new angle means the bear can get its teeth around the dog. One bone crushing bite and the last dog lies still on the ground.

As soon as you see the bear stand up again you hastily step backwards and blend into the crowd. You haven't won anything but at least if you keep your head down you won't lose anything either. Time to eat.

Turn to page 7.

You try to grab your money pouch back but one of the men holds you by the arms. The leader beckons for your money pouch. He slices it open with a small eating knife and gropes around inside. You watch his mouth gradually turn up into a smile as he lays his hands on the twenty silver pennies that you won at the bear baiting.

"This is our lucky day... and your lucky day peasant," spits the leader. "Come on boys, the Gnarly Goat awaits!" The soldiers quickly lose interest in you and cheer raucously.

"By the grace of King Henry you will live... for today," proclaims the leader staring hard at you. Then he too loses interest and they all stomp off down towards the town centre for a night of drunkenness at the inn.

Turn to page 72.

26

In the end your belly makes the decision for you. You can't turn down the offer of food and drink when you are so hungry.

The old woman leads you down a winding path through the trees until, an hour or two later, you arrive at a crooked old cottage. The cottage is constructed in the typical medieval fashion – wattle and daub – a mix of mud, straw and urine used to create strong, insulated walls.

You enter the cottage which consists of one room only. The old woman bends down to light the fire while you collapse in a wooden chair. So much walking!

Turn to page 107.

Ale is good! You signal to the bar wench for yet another flagon of ale. You are beginning to enjoy yourself now. It may be a bit dangerous but at least there's plenty of action to keep you entertained.

You watch as the locals crowd around Gwynn, all curiosity and questions.

"Where exactly did you see this apparition?" a young farmer asks.

"Did it speak to you? Was it the ghost of the Virgin Mary?" squeals an ancient bent old man. Gwynn seems happy with all the attention. After a theatrical pause, he begins to answer the torrent of questions.

You listen carefully, and as you guessed, it was you arriving in the time machine that he must have seen, luckily from afar. You lean forward suddenly as you hear something very interesting.

"And..." Gwynn's eyes open wide, "that wasn't the only flash I saw this day. Just a few moments later I saw a second flash, similar to the first, but this time it came from the main chimney of the castle!" Satisfied, he sits back in his chair and gulps his ale.

A second flash! That means the time machine has re-located to a different spot, and now you know where it is! But, of all the places it could have re-located to, it had to be the castle... a place built to keep people out!

Turn to page 68.

28

You follow the brook for a few hours then you stumble upon a well-trodden path. You have a long last drink then leave the brook in order to follow the path. The path is wide and looks to be in daily use although it seems deserted right now.

From a young age you have always read books about the medieval days. You read that forests covered most of the land and that they were havens for outlaws and could be very dangerous.

You are not so sure though.

You've been walking for ages and you've seen nobody. You're even feeling a bit bored and worried that you'll never find your way out and will have to live in the trees for the rest of your life!

Turn to page 95.

You stare around you fidgeting nervously. She's only an old woman but with that knife in her hand, you don't stand a chance. You also suspect that she's not as frail as she makes out.

"His hair is... err... raven black," you mutter unconvincingly. She stands still in front of you for a few tense moments. Then all hell breaks loose.

"Liar... you filthy liar!" she screams. "You've never met my son." She swipes the knife at you, just missing your neck. It's time to get away from this crazy witch.

You turn and start to run but immediately trip over a tree root hidden in the grass. With a gasp you fall forward onto your face. Before you even have time to roll over, she is on top of you.

"Spy!" she screeches whilst stabbing at you with the long bladed knife. You manage to dodge the first few strikes but she fights like a rabid dog. It's only a matter of time before she plunges the knife into your chest. With her stench filling your nostrils, the last thing you hear is your own breath escaping through the hole in your lungs.

The End

Peering over the heads of a large rowdy circle of onlookers you see an enormous bald-headed bear rearing up on its hind legs and growling. A few feet from the bear is a pack of four vicious, snarling dogs being held back from the bear by a chain. A big man with a heavily scarred face and beard is stepping from person to person taking bets. You realise that when the whistle is blown, the dogs and the bear will be released and a fight to the death will commence.

The bear is enormous and looks like it has survived many a fight before but the dogs are drooling through their razor sharp teeth and almost breaking the chain in anticipation. The big scarred man arrives at your place in the circle.

"If you watch, you gotta put money down little one," he growls. "What's your bet? The dogs or the bear? Twenty silver pennies to the winner."

You haven't got enough money on you to pay back if you lose, but winning twenty silver pennies could really come in useful later. You decide to risk it!

If you bet on the bear, turn to page 63.

If you bet on the dogs, turn to page 24.

The boar focuses its wrath on the cause of its injury – you – then charges.

You try to side-step but one of its tusks catches you in the thigh and your leg collapses under you. Half crawling and dragging your injured leg across the path, you look around you, preparing for the next attack.

A few feet to your left you spot the low hanging branch of a tree. *If you can just pull yourself up out of harm's way...*

With one arm hooked over the branch you begin to pull. You get your other arm over the branch – nearly there. Then, with an angry squeal, the boar smashes into your back and your arms slip from the branch. There is a sudden splitting pain in the back of your head and everything goes black.

Turn to page 114.

Looking down at the ground, you mumble something about not being very hungry and that you are in a hurry and must go. The old woman grabs you by the wrist, hard.

"You kissed me! You kissed me and now you want to leave me, just like that?" she croaks. You yank your arm away. At least you're stronger than her.

"I *have* to go," you shout as you walk away from the forest clearing. With a piercing screech she suddenly lunges at you with her sharp dirty nails. Luckily you jump out of the way in time. Now you decide to run.

This woman is crazy!

You easily escape from the old woman, who is throwing stones at you and screaming, but escaping from the dark forest is another matter.

After a few more hours of walking, you are absolutely starving. You stumble on, under the forbidding boughs of the giant trees. You listen for the sound of horsemen or foraging peasants, anyone who could offer you a bite to eat. But you are all alone. A few weeks later, the sharpest eyed travellers notice a human skeleton sitting forlornly under an old oak tree.

The End

She is an old woman but with that long knife in her hand, you don't stand a chance. You also suspect that she's a lot stronger than she makes out. The old woman stares into your eyes as you think hard. *She* has got white hair so maybe her son has the same hair colour.

"His hair is white as snow," you state confidently. The old woman says nothing. She just stares at you in silence. You glance nervously at her knife, then at her face. She smiles knowingly for a second. You let out a breath and relax. Then... all hell breaks loose.

"Liar, you dirty little liar!" she screams, slashing at you with the knife. You manage to break away from her and start running towards the trees.

"Spy!" she screeches after you. Almost in the trees now, you turn your head to see if she is following you. To your surprise, you see her lean back and skilfully throw the knife in a perfect arc, right at you!

You turn back and jump for the trees when you feel a sharp stabbing pain in your back. She's hit you! You topple to the ground, unable to breathe. The last thing you know before you lose consciousness is the rancid smell of the old woman as she crouches down next to you and begins to search through your pockets.

The End

34

As you tentatively step out into the moonlight, you are immediately spotted by one of the men.

"Oi," he calls, "who goes there?" You hold out your hands to show that you mean no harm and begin to explain that you are searching for something and need help.

The men, who you now see are soldiers, crowd around you. A great hulking brute with the back of his head cleanly shaven pushes through to the front.

"Well, we are searching for something too," he says with a sneer. "We've heard tell of spies in this town, enemies of the great King Henry, and in particular, a certain knight by the name of Sir Donald."

Oh no! These are Henry's men, the bully boys that everyone here seems to hate. And they're hunting for Sir Donald!

Turn to page 92.

The thought of being trained as a squire and later a knight sounds amazing... but you miss your family and friends and can't help feeling sad. The only thing that will make you happy is to find that time machine and get back to your time, your century.

You pluck up the courage and tell the king that you're awfully sorry but you will be making a long journey and will have to turn his offer down. The king looks disappointed for a moment then his old creased face relaxes into a smile.

"I understand: once a traveller, always a traveller. May the wind always be at your back, and may your road lead you to fortune and fulfilment. Now is the time for feasting!"

You are relieved. He really *is* a good king.

Turn to page 124.

36

You all look alert as the sound of hoof beats draws near. A moment later a lone knight comes galloping around the bend swinging a massive broadsword.

Your companions barely get the chance to react as the lone knight scythes into them like a tornado, cutting them down one after another. There's something familiar about this knight but you can't put your finger on it.

You stand dumbfounded staring around at the twitching bloody corpses of Henry's men as the knight reins in his horse and takes off his helmet to reveal long golden hair.

"Pray tell me you are unhurt fair maiden?" he takes the princess' hand and gives it a chivalrous kiss. The princess blushes.

Turn to page 78.

You lift the rock with both hands grunting with the effort. Stepping towards the wild boar you take aim at its head. The boar ignores you, its snout still to the ground hunting for food.

You throw the rock as hard as you can, almost losing your balance. The rock sails through the air but comes crashing down on the boar's rump. The boar squeals with rage and hops around in a circle lashing out at everything it sees.

Then it turns its beady little eyes on you.

You are no jungle trekker; you've just infuriated the poor beast!

Turn to page 31.

38

Feeling guilty about escaping through the window during the night, you tell the old woman that you have indeed met her son Sir Donald. She lets out a whoop of delight. You think to yourself that she must be very proud of him and happier still if she meets someone who knows him.

Just as you are expecting more tales of her son's bravery and exploits, a deadly serious look comes into her eyes.

"How do I know you're telling the truth?" She stops suddenly and stares at you. "How do I know you're not a spy for the enemy? They would do anything to get their evil hands on my Donald. He's been undercover recruiting new soldiers for the good king for quite a while now," she divulges.

Turn to page 73.

You place the money carefully on the grass next to the wagon and step back.

"Pleasure doing business with you," calls the physician. You stand there for a moment not sure what to do. "Well, goodbye," he calls again, his voice sounding impatient.

You walk away slowly with the bottle in your hand. *Well, why not?* It can't do any harm.

You pour the contents of the bottle down your throat. Urrgh, it tastes horrible! *What a rude man*, you think to yourself. Why did he make you leave the money on the grass? And why did he hide behind his curtain the whole time? Oh well, maybe he thought you were an outlaw and wanted to rob him or maybe it's just the medieval custom.

You cough violently into your sleeve and stumble on down the forest path.

Turn to page 113.

40

Trusting your impulses you crouch low and creep up to the moving cart. You glance over at the driver. Luckily she's staring straight ahead so you pull yourself up into the cart and quickly cover yourself with straw.

You observe the driver from your hiding place. She is dressed in typical medieval peasant's clothing: a cheap woollen 'kirtle' dyed a greyish-blue colour and a tight-fitting brown cap. She looks middle-aged and has a plain but friendly face. As you watch her, she stares straight ahead and seems lost in her own thoughts.

You realise with a start that you have no idea where this cart is going but something... maybe your instincts, told you to hide here.

Turn to page 127.

You all turn to the girl, smiling savagely. You are beginning to enjoy the life of a bandit! Then, without warning the girl draws a knife from her saddle and throws it at the rat-faced soldier, your leader. It thuds into his throat and he crumples to the ground with a grunt.

"One more move and we kill you," you shout, pulling her down from the horse and passing her to the remaining three men to tie up.

You rip open the heavy-looking saddlebags and gasp as gold reflects in your eyes... a lot of gold. "Who are you to have such riches?" you ask.

"I am the daughter of King Edward and rightful princess of this realm," she spits at you. "When my father hears of this there will be hell to pay."

With all this gold and a princess as your prisoner things are definitely looking up for you!

Turn to page 122.

You didn't like the look in her eye as she made the drinks and you certainly don't recognise the smell of the herbs, although they do smell tasty.

"No thank you," you say politely. "I'm not thirsty." The old woman looks put out.

"Oh come on child," she croaks. "It won't kill you!"

"Err... I know, but no thanks all the same," you reply.

The old woman becomes strangely irritated. She stares at you for a moment then her face twists up with anger.

"I help you. I bring you back to my home. I make you a lovely crackling fire to warm your bones... and what thanks do I get?" she says, as she paces around the room. Screeching in rage, she adds, "None, only suspicion and distrust!"

Turn to page 65.

You don't feel safe here and decide that it's better to miss an opportunity for pleasant conversation than risk losing your head! You shin up the nearest tall tree and stay hidden high up in the branches while the horsemen come galloping around the bend.

From your hiding place you see that the horsemen are soldiers. They are heavily armoured and carry swords and bows. They definitely don't seem the friendly type.

You wait until the sound of hoof beats has died away then you climb down carefully and continue the way you were going. You decide to keep your ears open and your eyes peeled from now on.

Turn to page 104.

You sit up in your bed at home. The first thing you do is cough. Your head still hurts terribly too. You rub your eyes, confused. *Was it all just a dream?*

"Come on, time for college," shouts your mother up the stairs. "You're not getting out of school *that* easily."

After a few hours of school you are rushed immediately to hospital. At first the doctors look confused, then they begin to argue amongst themselves and demand to know where you've been. You tell them that you can't remember anything.

By now, ugly black growths cover your body and you are coughing up blood. The last thing you remember is seeing the panicked look in the doctors' eyes as they hover around your bed wearing masks.

Your school and family are quarantined just a few hours too late.

A few weeks later and the front page headline in all the newspapers reads:

WORLDWIDE PLAGUE PANDEMIC:
MILLIONS DIE!
*HOW THE MEDIEVAL PLAGUE RETURNED
REMAINS A MYSTERY...*

The End

You keep running for an hour or so then sit down breathless in the shade of the trees. You wipe the sweat off your forehead. *What a mad old crone!*

Anger builds up inside you. You've wasted a whole afternoon with the old woman when you should have been looking for the time machine.

There's something else. You are not feeling too well. In fact with every hour that passes you feel worse. Oh well, it doesn't matter. You feel OK to walk and that's the main thing. A quick coughing fit passes then you pull yourself to your feet and start walking.

The musty smell of the medieval forest surrounds you and chinks of sunlight glitter through the canopy.

Your ears prick up at the tinkling of bells, but before you can hide, a coloured wagon pulled by a dog-eared old mule comes rattling around the corner. *'Barber Surgeon and Respected Physician'* reads the blue lettering along the side of the wagon.

At last you're having some good luck for a change – a doctor! You flag him down.

Turn to page 61.

46

The congregation are gaping at you in complete horror. The priest storms down the aisle and grabs you sharply by the wrist. "What Devil's work is this? I hear music playing but without instruments," he roars.

You try to explain, even holding up the watch so he can see it but this only makes him gasp and take a step back. "This... this abomination is not of God. Only the Devil can make music inside one's head."

Realising the severity of the situation you try to run but the town guards catch you in the doorway and lead you to a small dank cell down in the town. Great – how are you going to find the time machine now?

Turn to page 101.

Right, that's it. It's time to leave. The inn is becoming a bit rowdy and you are beginning to have trouble getting up from your seat! Eventually you manage to rise and make straight for the bar to pay old Barnaby the innkeeper.

He appears like a genie, sweating and rubbing his hands together. You throw most of the pennies you have onto the bar. Barnaby counts out enough to pay for the ales that you drank but you are feeling strangely generous.

"You're the best innkeeper in the land Mr B," you slur, putting your arm around Barnaby. "Keep the change." Barnaby grins like a Cheshire cat and doesn't need to be told twice. He scoops up the money and yells at the bar wench. She comes bustling over with some bread and cheese for you.

"That's on the house," smiles Barnaby. You wolf down the food hungrily and feeling much steadier, head to the door. As you are stepping out into the sunlight and the sounds of the fair, you feel a chubby hand touch your arm. It's Barnaby again. He hands you a folded piece of paper, gives you a conspiring wink, then turns back into the inn. You immediately unfold the note. *Bet on the bear. It's fixed,* the note reads. The bear? Fixed? You have no idea what it means.

Turn to page 111.

48

You rub your eyes and look around. To your surprise you are in your bed at home. Sunlight beams through the curtains and you realise it is morning. A familiar shout comes from downstairs.

"Come on, get out of bed. School starts in half an hour and you haven't even eaten your breakfast yet."

"OK, I'll be down in a minute," you shout back. You drag yourself out of bed and start getting dressed. *Was it all just a dream?* You still feel full from all the feasting. The last thing you want is breakfast!

A minute later and your mother's voice bellows up again from the kitchen.

"I hope you've revised for your exam today... You didn't forget did you?" *Exam?* You had completely forgotten.

"What exam?" you call back feeling worried.

"History," she replies. "Today is your final exam on medieval history."

You can't help grinning to yourself. Medieval history? Somehow you know that you are definitely going to get an A!

Congratulations!
You managed to safely return to your own time.

The End

Passing through the studded wooden doors your nose is assailed by the smell of incense. You stare up at the freshly cut stone of the ceiling vault. *These old churches were actually brand new at one time!* The pews are packed with grim-faced parishioners and the priest is droning on about a 'grave new punishment from God which comes from the south'. You take a seat and listen.

"Beware, for our sins are being punished; hell has come to Earth. Word reaches us from the south that the Lord has sent a miasma, a pestilence that kills in days... we must all repent!"

A miasma? What is he talking about? You hope that you will be long gone by the time any 'pestilence' reaches this town.

Your thoughts are interrupted by a peculiar sound – *beep-beep, beep-beep.* The priest stops talking and the entire congregation turns to stare at you. *What?*

Now the *beep-beep* has become a tune: a digital beeping version of 'Happy Birthday'. You pull up your sleeve to see your wrist watch flashing the word 'alarm' on a tiny digital screen. You hurriedly switch it off and look up smiling. "Don't worry, it's only my..." you begin, until you see the look on everyone's face.

Turn to page 46.

50

"Shut your mouth," you reply. "What am I? A performing monkey?" A collective gasp comes from the soldiers and they all turn to Henry. Henry jumps up and steps towards you whilst calmly unsheathing his sword. Oops, you've done it now. You don't stand a chance!

The men are all smiling, eager for your blood to flow. Henry points the sword at your face then lowers the blade, first touching one shoulder, then the other. "You have spirit young one," he says. "Spirit should not be wasted so hastily. With this sword I declare you one of us."

It seems he likes your tone and now the men get up one by one and slap you on the back laughing. You are now one of Henry's men!

After feasting and a good night's sleep among the trees you arise to your first day's work, robbing travellers.

Turn to page 112.

You signal for more ale. Much safer to just relax in the corner and keep an ear open. The argument is now getting a bit heated.

"So, you're calling me a fool eh?" shouts Leofric, drawing his sword and kicking over the nearest table.

"Calm down man!" pleads Barnaby the innkeeper, sweating and looking decidedly worried. "We're all friends here."

You watch the customers of the Gnarly Goat begin to get up and stand behind little Gwynn as if they are all on his side. Listening, you learn that Leofric is one of Henry's men. This Henry is apparently claiming the throne as his own and enforces his power with violence. You can see that the locals are against Henry and listening further you hear that they hope the good King Edward drives out the enemy and reclaims what is rightfully his.

Leofric is now outnumbered. He angrily sheaths his sword and pushes his way through the throng of locals towards the door. "Henry will hear of this," he growls. "I'll have you all executed for heresy!" He stomps out into the street.

If you decide to drink up and explore the fair, turn to page 118.

If you're in no rush and decide to have another ale, turn to page 27.

You tell the old woman that you have no idea who her son is. She looks surprised.

"You live here and you've never heard of Sir Donald?" she says, peering up at you suspiciously. You decide to change the subject quickly, before she asks more questions and realises that you are definitely not local.

"Wow, I'm so hungry," you groan. "I've been lost in this forest for ages and have barely eaten anything."

"You poor dear," she says. "I'll show you the way to the town, and there you will find an inn."

At last you emerge from under the dark canopy of the forest.

In the distance you can see a small town. It must be the same town you saw when you first arrived in the time machine, but seen from a different angle. You both walk down a grassy hillside and from your elevated position you can see that a fair is in town today.

Turn to page 53.

As you enter the narrow streets of the village you stop under the large hanging sign of an inn that creaks as it swings in the breeze. The inn is called the Gnarly Goat. The sign depicts an old, grinning, one-legged goat standing upright and leaning on a walking stick.

The shouts of men and the scents of sweat and ale waft out from the wooden door.

"Must be off dear, shopping to do." The old woman turns and shuffles away in the direction of the fair.

Turn to page 21.

54

You watch Sir Donald walk away towards the stables.

Standing in the centre of the castle courtyard you observe the young squires practising their swordplay. It looks as though they are fighting for real, although you know they are just training. There are chickens and pigs wandering loose, all making a cacophony of sounds.

You stroll around for a while observing the castle life.

Looking up you count numerous archers on the ramparts waxing their bowstrings and chatting. You step aside as a wealthy-looking lady strides haughtily past you accompanied by a gaggle of maid servants who are all trying to braid her hair as she walks. The kitchens are too hot to even go inside but the smells of the various meats, roasting ready for tonight's feast, make your mouth water.

Turn to page 70.

You rise to your feet and proudly declare, "Long live King Henry." The room falls silent. Sir Donald's face is a picture of shock and surprise.

"Henry?" he bellows. "You come to my house, drink my wine and all the time you are a spy!" You put up your hands innocently and try to explain.

"I...I didn't know," you stutter. "I'm not a spy... really."

"Liar," booms Sir Donald. "You are loyal to that dog. I heard it from your very lips!"

The next thing you know Sir Donald is reaching for his sword. Before you can dodge out of the way, he brings the hilt of it crashing down upon your head. You come round a few hours later, still on the floor of the house. You see the night sky through the windows. When you try to move, you realise that your arms and legs are tied up. Sir Donald returns and informs you that in the morning you will be taken to King Edward and tried for treason. No amount of pleading from you will change his mind.

The usual punishment for treason is death by hanging or beheading so you don't have much hope. But maybe you'll be lucky enough to spend the rest of your life in a dirty, cold medieval dungeon.

The End

56

The horse hurtles around the next bend to reveal a peculiar scene in the road ahead.

The source of the scream is a young lady dressed in fine clothes. She is being held to the ground by three rough-looking men who are struggling to tie her arms and legs. You also notice two dead soldiers and a small rat-faced man with a dagger in his throat all lying in the mud. The men look like outlaws and you realise that a robbery is taking place. Not for long though!

Sir Donald screams like a banshee giving the outlaws just enough warning to glance up before he smashes into them like a freight train. You grip Sir Donald's back squeezing your eyes shut as he whirls his sword around him cutting into the surprised outlaws without mercy.

Turn to page 82.

You trot down the muddy path towards the small medieval town a mile or so away. As you enter the narrow streets everything seems quiet, too quiet. It's then that you walk around a corner and see why. There's a fair in town today. The centre of the town is empty but the surrounding fields are now filled with market stalls and crowds of people.

You walk in the direction of the fair but stop under the large hanging sign of an inn that creaks as it swings in the breeze. The inn is named the Gnarly Goat. The sign depicts an ancient, grinning, one-legged goat standing upright and leaning on a walking stick like an old man. The chattering of men and the reek of sweat and ale wafts out from the wooden door.

If you think that a pint of ale in the Gnarly Goat and a chat with the locals could help your mission, turn to page 21.

If you're not thirsty and decide it's better to get straight to the fun of the fair, turn to page 111.

58

You take the steaming cup from her hands and thank her politely. The herbal brew tastes like it smells, delicious. You gulp it down eagerly and sit back in the chair. You are definitely feeling more relaxed.

"You know, I always wanted to have more children," the old woman sighs, smiling fondly at you, "a child who actually cares for me, a child who doesn't run off to fight wars, a child who would never leave their old mother alone."

She leans closer to you.

Turn to page 83.

You rise to your feet and proudly declare, "Long live King Edward." The room falls silent for a few moments then Sir Donald rests a hand on your shoulder.

"Ah, a warrior of truth and honour. Brave and stout of heart I daresay," he sighs contentedly. "Forgive me for doubting your honour. These are times of distrust and suspicion."

Phew! You said the right thing. It seems Sir Donald thinks of you as one of his own. It could be very useful to have a knight as your friend in this dangerous world. Sir Donald informs you that tomorrow he will take you to the castle to meet the good King Edward.

"The king is always in need of more servants," he says. "Do not fear. I will find you work and a place to live."

Turn to page 76.

60

You get dressed in your modern replica medieval clothes and step out to the kitchen where Sir Donald is still chatting away.

"Being such a beautiful day I must pay a visit to someone before taking you to the castle," he tells you. "My mother is none too healthy these past days and I would feel shameful if I didn't visit her. She lives out in the great forest. It is scarcely an hour's ride from here."

He finishes buckling on his armour and steps out onto the street. A moment later he reappears sat astride an enormous warhorse, every inch the classic medieval knight. "You may accompany me if you please or, if you prefer, I will return for you later."

You know you could use the precious time alone to search for the time machine in the town but sticking with Sir Donald could keep you out of danger.

If you jump up onto the horse and go with Sir Donald to the forest on the way to the castle, turn to page 17.

If you wait for Sir Donald to pick you up later and take the opportunity to search for the time machine in the town, turn to page 110.

The wagon comes to a halt and a bald-headed, stern-looking face peeps out from behind a curtain.

"Can I help you young traveller?" he says in a strict voice that reminds you of a school teacher. "Well?" he says poking his head out further from his wagon.

"Hello, I'm not feeling well at all," you tell him. "This morning I was fine, but now I feel terrible." Without warning you break into another intense fit of coughing. Seeing this, the physician immediately disappears back behind the curtain.

Was it your imagination or did you catch a look of fear on his face?

"I have just the thing," he yells from inside the wagon. "It's called Cure-all Physic, a modern miracle of medicine."

A small bottle appears on the ledge of the wagon and the physician's hand darts back behind the curtain.

Turn to page 62.

You peer at the strange label. Judging by the list of ailments that it cures it really does seem a miracle of modern medicine.

"It's 4 pence a bottle," comes the hidden voice again. "Guaranteed success within three days or your money back!"

You know you have enough pennies but are just wondering how you *would* actually go about claiming your money back when the stern voice yells again. "Come on, I'm in a hurry. Leave the money on the grass and let's be done with it."

If you buy the Cure-all Physic, turn to page 39.

If you prefer not to buy the medicine, turn to page 12.

The bear is gigantic and it *does* look pretty mean. The bear has got to win, you decide. The chains are cut and the fight begins.

The first dog jumps straight at the bear but before its muzzle even gets within biting distance the bear whacks it out of the way with the swipe of a huge paw, opening its belly all over the grass. The next two dogs jump together. One of them, a skinny black dog with one ear, gets a grip on the bear's flank. It holds on for a few seconds then the bear rolls onto its side and crushes both dogs instantly. You wince at the sickening crunching sound.

Now the last dog – a big brute of a dog, orange and black with teeth like a shark! It growls deep in the back of its throat and jumps. The bear is caught around the neck by the dog's massive jaws. After a few tense seconds of flailing around, the bear falls forward but the new angle means the bear can get its teeth around the dog. One bone crushing bite and the last dog lies still on the ground.

You saunter off with a cheeky smile and twenty silver pennies jangling in your pocket! Time to eat.

Turn to page 7.

64

You're not going to let anyone boss you around!

You give the hooded stranger a vicious kick to the shin and when you feel his grip loosen on your shoulder you kick him again for good measure then make a run for it without looking back.

You dash back past the food stalls, push your way through the crowd watching the next bear baiting of the day and vanish back into the narrow streets of the town.

Turn to page 99.

You sit there in the chair dumbfounded. This woman is totally crazy!

"If you don't drink that brew... I'll... I'll..." she turns to you and whips out a long wicked knife from her skirts.

"Right, I'm off," you shout, and jump out of the chair and through the door before she can catch you. It's lucky she's old and frail.

You look back at the cottage and to your surprise you see her lurch out of the door; she's chasing you! Luckily you are way ahead, so you run and run through the forest until the mad screeches disappear into the distance.

Turn to page 45.

You head down into town and directly to Sir Donald's house. You really hope he won't be angry that you ran away from him in the middle of the night. You knock on his door.

"Well, well, if it isn't the midnight wanderer!" bellows Sir Donald opening the door. "I was worried. I made a silent vow to protect you, you know."

"Uh... I'm sorry," you stammer. "Also, I think I met your mother."

"My mother?" he seems surprised. "You're lucky to still be here!" You're not totally sure what he means but she *was* a bit crazy. He continues, "I have not visited her for a long while. She can be a dangerous woman." He gives you a probing look. It's almost as if he is examining you. A moment passes and the lines on his face relax. He instructs you to wait there, then returns moments later on the back of an enormous warhorse. Dressed in chain mail and a multi-coloured over-garment with a broadsword at his hip, he certainly does look a picture. You can't help grinning.

"No time to waste, jump on and we'll be off to the castle." Sir Donald pulls you up into the saddle behind him and you saunter off happily into the countryside.

Turn to page 75.

You feel honoured and accept the king's offer without hesitation. Sir Donald grins at you. You have made him proud. You sit down with the king and Sir Donald.

Over the next few hours you eat more than you've ever eaten before. Fat stuffed birds of all kinds, sweet meats cooked with fruit, extravagant artistic dishes, all washed down with wine and mead.

King Edward tells you of the invader King Henry and how his bullying soldiers are running amok over his once peaceful lands. Tomorrow you will go to the armoury to be measured for your chain mail and weapons and your training will begin!

At first you miss your family and friends from the twenty-first century. You miss electricity, running water and television. But, as the years roll by, you forget how to even pronounce these strange foreign words. You live a lifetime of chivalry. Defending the lands from enemies and eventually marrying and gaining lands of your own.

A stone effigy of you is sculpted upon your death at an old age, and hundreds of years later, tourists still visit the cathedral where you lie, wondering aloud to each other... 'Who was this brave knight?'

The End

Smiling to yourself, you guzzle down the rest of your flagon and slam it down on the sturdy oak table. Now you know where to find the machine and your only way back to the present: your family and friends, cars, electricity and mobile phones. Gazing around the room you think to yourself that these people have family and friends but none of the modern electrical gadgets that you are used to... but they seem content enough. The voice of a burly young farmer rises above the mutterings of the locals. He is singing a jolly drinking song and before you know it, everybody is joining in, flagons swinging and spilling all over the straw-covered floor.

> *"We hold it up, we drink it down,*
> *It makes the room go round and round..."*

An old woman lets slip a thunderous burp and everybody laughs heartily. You realise that the song is right. When you concentrate hard, you can actually feel the room spinning round and round! You stare at your flagon for a few moments before you realise it's empty again.

If you signal for more ale, turn to page 100.

If you decide enough is enough and stagger out into the fresh air, turn to page 47.

You glance down at the knife. Sweat begins to break out on your brow. You *have* met Sir Donald before but what colour hair did he have? Then it comes to you, of course, the day he threw back his hood at the fair. His ginger hair looked golden under the afternoon sun.

"His hair is like golden sun," you say confidently.

The old woman eyes you for a second then the knife disappears back where it came from, in a flash.

"Forgive me child, I am overburdened with fear and suspicion..." she sighs then adds sadly, "I am burdened with many evils." *Evils?* You're not sure what she means by that but she's definitely unstable! She sits down on the grass and appears to be weeping softly.

"Well, I really must return to your son now," you murmur not wanting to interrupt.

Turn to page 97.

Thinking of the feast, you decide to make your way to the great hall located in the central keep. Being the strongest part of the castle, the keep only has one small heavy door.

As you approach, the two guards look up at you and start laughing. You wish you had researched the latest fashion before you travelled back here. The tallest guard speaks.

"Do you think we're going to let you in 'ere to dine with His Majesty wearing that!" he laughs.

Both guards then become serious and cross their spears across the entrance.

"You may enter if you can solve this riddle," says the tall guard.

"There are one hundred houses in a street and a man must paint the number of the house (1 to 100) on each front door.

The riddle is this: how many times will the man paint the number nine during this task?"

Turn to the page that corresponds to the answer.

After the meal you return to your tiny room. Looking out of the window you see that you are in a large stone monastery at the top of a gentle slope. The sun reflects off a small shiny object on the roof below. Someone must have thrown it out of the window. Reaching down from the window you scoop up an empty packet that once contained pills. Red letters on the side read 'Antibiotics'. *How?* You know you didn't bring any with you so how can these medieval monks have access to modern antibiotics?

Some instinct tells you to check your trouser pocket and to your horror it's empty. The return device has gone!

You groan and sit back on the bed holding your aching head. That's why Brother Hector's powers of healing are second to none. He's secretly using antibiotics. And if he's using antibiotics he must be from the future too! So you're not the first person to be sent back in time. The scientists lied.

You have already guessed that Brother Hector stole your return device from your trousers when you were unconscious, to save himself and return to the future, meaning you are stuck here in his place.

Maybe the scientists will send someone else in six months and you can steal *their* return device?

The End

You are angry for losing your two-hundred-florin winnings but who knows what may have happened if you'd had nothing to steal?

Just then an old wooden cart pulled by an ox creaks by. It is full to the brim with straw. Looking off to your left you can see the edge of the enormous forest that surrounds the town. You also feel a bit bad about Sir Donald. What will he do when he wakes up in the morning to find you are not there?

If you leap into the back of the cart and cover yourself with straw, turn to page 40.

If you are curious to see what lies within the dark forest, turn to page 5.

If you decide to creep back into Sir Donald's house and pretend you've been asleep all the time, turn to page 94.

The old crone looks you up and down for a moment. Then, before you can blink, she whips out a cruel looking knife from under her skirts. Holding the knife expertly, her wrinkled lips begin to move with a haunting melody:

> *"Golden sun,*
> *Raven black,*
> *Or locks as white as snow.*
> *If truth you speak,*
> *The colour of his hair,*
> *You would surely know."*

If you say his hair is golden sun, turn to page 69.

If you say his hair is raven black, turn to page 29.

If you say his hair is white as snow, turn to page 33.

You decide that it's a better idea to stay hidden in the cart and risk capture. Anyway, you'd never get away without being seen from those giant stone walls.

You keep your head down under the straw as the cart rumbles over the wooden drawbridge. Looking up, you see the wicked-looking spikes of the iron portcullis overhead.

You think back to good old Sir Donald. You remember that he was going to bring you to this castle the morning after you jumped out of his window. Hopefully he wasn't angry when he woke up to find you had gone!

Turn to page 115.

Sir Donald keeps the horse at a steady trotting pace. You gaze at the passing countryside. The fields are full of people. Some are farmers sweating over the heavy ploughs pulled by oxen. Others toil away in enormous communal fields working off the time that they owe to their lords. Eventually you look up and see the giant intimidating castle walls looming over you. You cross a short drawbridge and the sleepy-looking guard at the main gate recognises Sir Donald at once.

"Greetings Sir Knight, your timing is uncanny. A grand feast will take place this very eve in the great hall." He laughs at Sir Donald and gives you a knowing wink as you pass under the wicked-looking portcullis. *Wow*, you are going to be feasting with the king!

You both dismount in the busy interior courtyard and Sir Donald leads the horse away, yelling for the stable boy.

"I have some business to take care of," he calls over his shoulder. "Be in the great hall at the setting of the sun."

"OK," you reply. That means you have about an hour to explore the castle.

Turn to page 54.

76

It seems Sir Donald thinks you are homeless and in need of help. Well, you *are* in need of help but you already have a home. Just not here in this time.

The cloak of night envelopes the land outside and you feel worn out.

"Come, sleep." Sir Donald leads you to a tiny but comfortable room adjacent to the main room with the fire. He then goes back to his chair by the fireside. Within minutes you can hear him snoring loudly.

You lie down and drift off to sleep thinking about what the day will hold tomorrow at the castle.

Turn to page 102.

She's no princess but if she really can help you, maybe it's worth it. You lean forward and purse your lips. The smell is suffocating – old sweat, garlic and mouldy onions. Now that you are closer to her, you notice strange black growths on her neck... urrgh disgusting! You peck her on the cheek and pull away quickly. A few tense seconds pass. The old woman's smile grows wider until she suddenly bursts out laughing.

"Ha ha," she cackles. "What are you waiting for? You think I'm going to turn into a frog or something?" You look confused. "This is no fairy tale child, this is real." She cackles louder.

You get the distinct feeling that this old crone is playing with you. Your face turns red and you start to walk away.

"Wait child," she says, her face now becoming deadly serious. "Let me take you to my humble cottage. I have food, wine and the fire is set."

If you think this old woman is mad and decide to get away while you can, turn to page 32.

If you decide that she's harmless and that you could really do with something to eat at her cottage, turn to page 26.

"I knew you would come to save me Sir Donald. My father will repay you generously," she says.

They both turn unfriendly faces towards you. "It was him; he's their leader," the princess points at you angrily. The knight dismounts holding a long iron chain then presses his face close to yours.

"You should have listened to me at the fair," he whispers. *The fair?* Of course, that's why he looks familiar; he was the cloaked man who was following you.

You feel the chain being locked around your arms and legs as the knight lifts you onto his horse. He looks at you sadly. "You shall have an eternity to think on your mistakes in the dungeons of King Edward's castle."

The End

You stand staring at the circle of gruff soldiers all waiting for you to sing. You suspect Henry is testing you. Maybe he is confused because he cannot guess where you are from and he wants you to prove it by singing a local song.

You think fast. 'Greensleeves' is the only song you know that is even vaguely medieval so immediately you launch into an improvised version of the song whilst dancing in what you believe to be a medieval style.

The men silently look from you to Henry waiting for their future king's reaction. A tense moment passes then Henry bursts out laughing. He falls back screaming with laughter and the men all join in. Embarrassed you stop singing and scowl at the men, which only serves to make them laugh harder.

Turn to page 15.

The sun begins its descent and the night draws in as you sit talking with Sir Donald. You learn that he is fighting for the freedom of the local folk, against a tyrant who claims to be king and who is robbing and pillaging the country for his own benefit.

Sir Donald looks pensive for a moment then jumps up with a start and eyes you suspiciously.

"I've told you all about my good self but what of *you* fair traveller? Be you a servant of honour, or be you a spy, a creature of the tyrant?" He leans towards you, glancing sideways at his sword. "Are you with King Henry or King Edward?"

If you stand up and declare, "Long live King Henry," turn to page 55.

If you stand up and declare, "Long live King Edward," turn to page 59.

Your logic tells you that if this knight wanted to do you harm, he could have done it anytime. You roll over and drift back to sleep, tangled in the warm woollen blankets.

Sunlight streams in between the opened shutters, and a plate of cheese and apples is thrust under your nose.

"A fine morning it is to be sure. Well rested I trust?" says a cheery Sir Donald. You nod your head, your mouth already stuffed with cheese. "Take your time. That cheese isn't going to grow legs and run away!"

Sir Donald chuckles and disappears through the door to fetch some ale.

Turn to page 60.

82

When you finally open your eyes you see unmoving bodies strewn all over the road. Sir Donald is puffing and panting. "Are you unhurt fair maiden?" he addresses the young lady.

"Valiant Sir Donald. You saved my life," she gasps dusting off her dress, "and who is this brave knight?" She tilts her head at you.

"I'm not really a knight," you mumble.

"Nonsense," she replies. "Come with me to the castle and you shall be a knight before this day is ended."

Sir Donald beams at you proudly.

"Go hither and protect this fair maiden on her journey home," he says. "I will rendezvous with you later after I have visited my mother."

Her journey home? Didn't she say, 'Come to the castle'?

Turn to page 16.

While she is talking, you feel more and more relaxed. In fact, when she leans closer, you find it impossible to move away. You begin to panic. You try to stand up, but your legs do not obey you.

"You would never leave your old mother alone, would you?" asks the old woman as she begins to stroke your hair.

You look over at the old woman's cup and to your horror you see that she hasn't touched it. It's then that it dawns on you. You have drunk a herbal mixture that paralyses your whole body.

The old woman is gazing at you with a loving smile. You realise that you are going to live there, trapped with her, forever.

"My child," she whispers lovingly in your ear. "You would never leave your old mother... would you?"

The End

You decide that it's better to wait and talk to them. You could ask for food, directions; anything is better than walking alone in a forest for days on end!

With a thunderous roar the horsemen come galloping around the bend. Immediately they rein in their horses and come to a halt. They look like soldiers. The leader holds up a gauntleted hand for silence.

"Long live King Henry!" he shouts, then stares at you. You're not sure what to do.

"Um, have you got any food?" you ask politely. The other soldiers begin to laugh and circle around you on their massive warhorses. You feel very intimidated.

"Our Lord Henry decrees that the forests should be cleared of vermin like you," smiles the leader menacingly. You hear a sudden 'twang' and a slicing pain in your back. Arrows! The soldiers continue to laugh as they use you for target practice.

You live just long enough to see the leader dismount and swing his sword in a perfect arc towards your neck.

The End

The unfamiliar voices and almost complete darkness begin to fill you with anxiety. Better to get back to a warm bed than wander alone out here in the night.

Keeping your head down you creep back around the corner and create some distance between you and the strangers before they notice you are there.

As quiet as a mouse you tiptoe up to the silhouette of Sir Donald's house. The shutters on your bedroom window are still partly open as you left them, so getting back inside should be easy.

Turn to page 125.

You have no idea who this man is but you decide to take a risk.

"OK, I'll come," you say, still a little unsure. The man grabs your wrist hard, and leads you to the other side of the fair. You are surrounded by multi-coloured tents. You see squires polishing their masters' armour or grooming enormous horses.

"There are those who would wish to rob you," the man whispers. "I've seen them watching you." The only person you've noticed watching you is him. *Maybe he's the one who wants to rob you?*

Just then he throws off his hood to reveal a handsome but scarred face. You notice an old sword wound like an ugly stripe down his cheek. What grabs your attention most is his long, flowing, ginger hair. It looks golden under the afternoon sun. You begin to speak, to ask him what the heck is going on, but he shoves his dirty hand over your mouth.

"Shh," he hisses. "Come, I'll take you to my hideout."

If you still trust this man and let him take you to his hideout, turn to page 123.

If you think it's a trap and decide to run for it, turn to page 18.

If the girl has a guarded escort, she, or something they are carrying, must be valuable! You decide to rob the girl.

After a few minutes the wagon has passed out of sight and the girl and her escort are directly below the overhanging branches of the tree where you are hiding. Your companions give the signal and you all jump down from the tree and attack the two guards. Surprised, the guards haven't even unsheathed their swords and are quickly overcome by Henry's cut-throats.

Turn to page 41.

You stare at the man seated to Sir Donald's left. He is a giant of a man and looking at his belly it's obvious that he eats well. He looks into your eyes with a warm smile.

It's the king, the good king!

"Enchanted to meet you young traveller," he says in a deep rich voice. "I've heard a lot about you." Embarrassed, you can only manage a smile. He continues. "Here, I am always looking for people of honour and stout heart to aid me in the many chores this kingdom demands of me."

He lays his hand upon your arm. "You would be doing me a great service if you were to live here and become a squire of my household." He looks at you expectantly.

If you accept this generous offer, turn to page 67.

If you risk refusing the king's offer, turn to page 35.

"How dare you rob an innocent old man!" cries a stern voice from below you inside the wagon.

By now the wagon is hurtling down the path and, looking back, you see your companions sprawled in the mud where they have fallen off. You alone hang on until at last the mule draws to a halt and starts munching the grass. *Right, it's time for you to impress your new friends.*

You draw your knife and drop down inside the wagon. Inside there are hundreds of bottles filled with strange liquids and animal parts preserved in jars. You spin around and come face to face with an old, bald and very angry-looking man. You pause for a second clutching your knife, building up the courage to rob your first ever victim, when a splash of cool liquid hits your face.

The physician is staring at you in horror holding a, now empty, glass bottle. You smile. *A splash of water won't stop me*, you think. That's when you hear the fizzing noise and feel the pain. Your whole face suddenly feels like it is burning. Glancing again at the empty bottle in the physician's hand you see the word 'acid' painted upon the label. Your first ever victim has become the last face you will ever see.

The End

Her smell is overpowering so you take a step back. There's no way on Earth you are going to kiss this sewer-scented crone, you decide.

Just then she bursts into a cackle of laughter.

"Ha ha, you're not as stupid as you look," she says. "The foolish always kiss me. They think I'm going to turn into a frog or something. This is no fairytale young'un!"

Oh, so she was trying to trick you, you realise. Well, at least you don't have to kiss her! The old woman rises from the tree stump, her old bones creaking. She tells you that this part of the forest is very near to a small village.

"Come, walk with me," she smiles and begins to shuffle off in the direction of the village. Why not, you decide. After all, you *can* run away whenever you want, and she seems to have a sense of humour.

Turn to page 96.

You decide to investigate. Gulping down the rest of your ale you rise from your stool.

"So, you're calling me a fool eh?" shouts Leofric, drawing his sword and kicking over the nearest table.

"Calm down man!" pleads Barnaby, sweating and looking decidedly worried. "We're all friends here." You pluck up the courage and step over towards the two men.

"Um, excuse me. I think I can explain the flash," you stutter nervously. "Also, I don't suppose any of you have seen a second flash around here?" you ask smiling politely. Gwynn looks shocked but backs off as the big bearded Leofric pushes you away roughly.

"So," he booms. "First you butt into a private conversation. Then claim *you* can explain God's work. This is heresy!"

"No, no... Um I didn't mean...," you begin, fear rising in your throat like bile.

"What?" growls Leofric. "The Devil got your tongue?" It is then you realise that Leofric still has his sword unsheathed and to your horror he puts the cold steel tip to your throat. This man wants an excuse to kill someone and it seems you've just taken Gwynn's place. With one final shout of 'heresy', Leofric pushes his sword through your neck and you are dead before you hit the floor.

The End

92

You quickly murmur that you've never heard of this knight and that you're not from around here.

Bad mistake.

They begin to shove you around asking questions. Your nostrils fill with their sweaty odour as you are pushed from one armoured hulk to the next. One of the soldiers then snatches your money pouch from you and holds it up triumphantly.

"There had better be something for us in here little one," the man glares at you.

If you won twenty silver pennies on the bear baiting, turn to page 25.

If you didn't win any money, turn to page 106.

You don't want to be trapped inside that castle and, looking at the size of the walls, you wouldn't be able to escape very easily once inside.

You slip silently out from underneath the straw and lie flat in the long grass while the cart rumbles over the drawbridge and out of sight. When the drawbridge is closed once more, you crawl around the side wall of the castle away from the prying eyes at the gate but, *too late!*

A shout comes from above you up on the ramparts. It's quickly followed by answering shouts and before you know it, arrows begin to thud into the ground all around you.

You think of standing up and calling out that you are a friend and mean no harm, but from your previous experiences you decide it's better to just try and escape.

Turn to page 98.

You are woken by the sunlight streaming in between the shutters to see Sir Donald standing over you with a bowl of pottage in his hands. He smiles.

"A good morning to you. Eat this, it'll warm the belly." You rub the sleep from your eyes and stare into the bowl.

"It looks like cooked leftovers," you say, before you remember your manners.

"That's because it is!" says Sir Donald briskly. "Come on, get your boots on, it's time to leave this place. Last night I heard soldiers shouting outside, quite the ruckus I daresay. It's not safe to delay. We must get straight to the castle."

You wonder if Sir Donald guesses that you ran off and were involved in the 'ruckus' last night.

Turn to page 116.

Just then you notice a distant sound – like thunder. You look up at the sky – no clouds.

A few seconds later and you realise the sound is getting nearer... fast. You can feel the ground rumbling now and looking down you see the many hoof prints already marked in the mud.

Of course, horses.

By the noise there must be twenty at least. They are only seconds from rounding the bend where you are standing.

If you climb the nearest tree and hide in the branches while the horsemen pass below you, turn to page 43.

If you wait on the path, turn to page 84.

As you walk she tells you about her son, Sir Donald. According to her, he is a famous knight.

"Never visits his old mother anymore," she sighs sadly. "He is always too busy saving damsels in distress and fighting evil."

She turns to you with a curious look in her eyes. "Have you met my son, Sir Donald?"

If you were at Sir Donald's house last night, turn to page 38.

If you have no idea who Sir Donald is, turn to page 52.

She grabs a stick and draws you a map in the earth. The map shows the forest path back to the town. You feel nervous with all this talk of evils, and after being threatened with a knife you are in no mood to hang around chatting.

You stride off towards Sir Donald's house and, looking back, see the old woman sitting on the ground singing softly to herself, as she was when you first met her.

When you jumped from Sir Donald's window last night you memorised his house number.

Turn to the page that corresponds to Sir Donald's house number.

You stay low and move closer to the castle walls to reduce the archers' line of sight. But you get a little too close and, scrambling for a handhold in the mud, fall into the castle moat. It's freezing and, even worse, it's disgusting! The water is a brownish-grey colour and is full of human waste and putrefied food from the kitchens.

You struggle to swim but the water is choking you. It fills your mouth and nose and you find it almost impossible to keep your head above the water. Under a rain of arrows you try desperately to pull yourself up the muddy banks of the moat but all your efforts are in vain.

The castle archers turn away and shrug as, at last, your body sinks below the dirty surface of the moat.

The End

You are just searching for a spot to stop and catch your breath when you hear a shout.

"Hey! That was a good kick."

A gang of four men step into view. "Bravo stranger," smiles the leader of the gang leaning on a barrel and clapping his hands slowly together. "I've been wanting to do what you just did for years! He's a dangerous one though, that cloaked man."

You stare at the men curiously. *Who are they?* Something tells you they are soldiers but they're wearing poor dirty clothes and they're not threatening you in any way.

"Come on, we're going to have some roast boar and a drop of wine," says the leader walking off up the street. He's a small fellow with a rat-like face but his companions are great hulking brutes. They must do all the fighting you think to yourself.

"Well?" calls the leader looking back at you over his shoulder. "Are you coming or not?"

Turn to page 128.

100

Why leave this fine inn? You have everything you need all around you. Fine ale, joyful song, medieval dancing... this is the life! You bash your flagon against the table until the bar wench strides over to you cursing and refills it. Ah... the nectar of kings!

After swigging down half the flagon you rise shakily to your feet and join in the dancing. Even Barnaby the innkeeper is up on the bar doing a kind of fat man's jig. You can't help grinning to yourself.

About an hour later you are sitting with some locals having an extremely in-depth conversation concerning the ways in which one could improve the town privy. That is about the last thing you remember before you fall off your stool with a grunt and a loud crash.

Turn to page 19.

The next morning you awaken to the stink of rotting straw and rat droppings. Before you have a chance to think, the guards come for you, leading you by a chain out into the town square.

Your mouth drops open when you see the wooden stake in the centre and the piled firewood all around it.

A multitude of townspeople are gathered to watch the burning. You are tied firmly to the stake and find yourself barely able to breathe. You can only listen in horror.

"In these trying times we must do all we can to root out the Devil and appease our Lord. The fact that this stranger can produce music without instruments is certain proof that the Devil resides within."

The priest from the church gestures towards you, his voice rising hysterically. "This wretched creature must be purified by fire," he shrieks as the flames begin to flicker at your feet. "May God have mercy upon your soul."

The End

102

You sleep fitfully. Tossing and turning you start to dream. You dream of televisions, cars, the Internet... you dream of fresh water readily available at the simple turn of a tap. You dream about your home and your family.

Waking with a start you realise that you miss the modern world, your world. Is this mysterious knight going to help you find the time machine and your way home or just hinder your progress?

You are feeling a little bit pressured by Sir Donald. *The king is always in need of more servants*, you remember him saying. You don't want to be somebody's servant! Then again, he does seem a noble character and you've been safe with him so far.

Turn to page 103.

Just then you notice, through a crack in the shutters, a tiny point of light dancing around outside. You lift yourself from the low wooden bed, rub the sleep from your eyes and peer out into the night. Yes, there is something out there; a glowing light that dances about and seems to be making its way towards the edge of town and the main tree line of the surrounding forest.

What can it be? A firefly? A forest spirit? It would only take a few minutes to satisfy your curiosity.

If you jump out of the window and investigate the strange light, turn to page 119.

If you decide it's safer to stay with Sir Donald and wait until the morning, turn to page 81.

You tramp on down the muddy path and now everything is silent again, except for your stomach which won't stop growling. Why didn't you bring any food?

A few moments later another sound attracts your attention; a loud rustle coming from beside the path. You stop and peer into a bush but are suddenly shoved to the ground as a squealing, bristle-covered shape bursts past you and out onto the path.

It's a wild boar!

It is bigger than a pig, with two mean-looking tusks jutting out from its hairy face. You jump up brushing dirt from your leggings. The boar starts sniffing around in the undergrowth searching for food. You're not the only hungry one! Next to you is a heavy grey rock. A crazy thought crosses your mind. Maybe it's just your survival instinct or something, but, couldn't you try and kill the boar for food? It always works for those jungle trekkers you see on TV.

Your mouth waters as a vision of the boar sizzling slowly over a blazing fire enters your head.

If you throw the rock at the boar and try to kill it, turn to page 37.

If you leave the boar and continue down the path, turn to page 14.

"Hello little one," you call in your 'kind' voice. "What's your name?" The girl's eyes open wide. It seems like she hasn't spoken to anyone in a while.

"Matilda," she mumbles.

"Well let's see if we can clean up that grubby face," you smile. You are just sliding from the horse's back when a hand firmly grips your arm. Sir Donald looks grim.

"Don't," he says.

"But... she's only little," you exclaim. "She needs our help."

Isn't Sir Donald supposed to be a chivalrous knight?

Turn to page 8.

The soldiers start laughing mockingly and throwing your money pouch between them. You try to snatch it back but it only seems to make them laugh harder. The big brute with the back of his head shaved grabs the pouch, tears it open with his bare hands and pours the contents onto the moonlit earth.

A couple of forgotten pennies and a dirty handkerchief are all that lie upon the ground.

"Is that it?" booms the shaven brute. "Is that all you have for your king's men, your protectors?" His face turns an ugly shade of purple and the other men look at you menacingly. He kicks away your pennies and your handkerchief then turns on you. Lifting you roughly by your neck, the leader spits in your face.

"You'd better have more than that or those pennies will pay for your grave." You can feel the fear rising in you. You don't have anything more.

"Umm... sorry," is about all you manage to whisper before feeling a heavy blow to your back. You scramble around on the ground searching desperately for somewhere to crawl away to, when the next blow comes. This time a metal gauntleted fist smashes down upon your head. You gasp once then everything goes black.

The End

A while later, and you and the old woman are sitting in front of a roaring fire. She tells you sadly of her son. According to her, he fights for the 'good' king and hasn't visited her for a long time.

"He's undercover," she confides. "He's forgotten all about his dear old mother."

Her face takes on a sad but strange look.

Suddenly she jumps up and goes to a big bubbling pot next to the fire. She takes two wooden cups and fills them from the pot. She then adds an array of herbs to the cups humming softly to herself. It smells delicious.

"After all that walking you must be tired. Drink this to restore your health." She offers you one of the cups.

If you thank the old woman and gulp down the brew, turn to page 58.

If you don't trust those herbs and refuse, turn to page 42.

108

Turning to your companions you whisper that the wagon is the best option. It could be holding a lot of gold and there don't appear to be any guards.

The girl passes under your tree unharmed but when the wagon passes under you a few minutes later, you all jump out of the tree with weapons drawn and murderous expressions on your faces.

"Halt in the name of the rightful King Henry," you shout landing with a *thump* on the roof of the wagon. You are expecting the 'respected physician' to be terrified but, to your surprise, he whips the mule into action and the wagon takes off at breakneck speed!

Turn to page 89.

Something tells you to trust Sir Donald. You throw your leg back over the horse and Sir Donald immediately whips it into a trot. You continue in sullen silence for a few minutes until Sir Donald finally speaks. "You must understand. There are rumours of a terrible new contagion that leaves none alive. Nobody is safe."

"Well, what makes you think that poor little girl was infected?" you ask.

"I recognise the symptoms," he replies. "I've... seen them before." You ask more questions but Sir Donald seems strangely preoccupied and will not speak further on the subject.

An hour passes under the eaves of the greenwood and you are wondering just how far away Sir Donald's mother lives when a female scream rings out across the forest. Sir Donald draws his broadsword and kicks the horse into a gallop.

"Hold on tight, keep your head down behind my back, and the armour will protect you," he calls to you over the thumping of the horse's hooves. You duck low trying to peer around Sir Donald to see where you are going. *What's happening?*

Turn to page 56.

110

You didn't travel back through time to go visiting sick medieval relatives. You've got a time machine to find.

As soon as the clip-clop of hooves is out of hearing you are straight out the door.

The townspeople are going about their daily business today now that the fair has moved on to the next town. You resist the inviting open door of the Gnarly Goat and head up a hill, crowned by a small stone church.

Turn to page 49.

You wander off through the streets away from the inn. You continue, weaving between the tightly packed houses, until you step out into the nearest field and enter the fair. All around you are strange sights, the medieval music of pipes and drums and the tempting aromas of food. You pass market stalls selling an array of strange smelling pasties and pies.

Up ahead on a small makeshift stage is a gaudily dressed minstrel singing a rather rude song about a rich lord and a farmer's daughter. The crowd are roaring with laughter and you suspect that the small weasely fellow you can see emptying their pockets is working together with the minstrel.

As you walk through an area filled with multi-coloured tents, you notice that a man from the minstrel's audience has broken away from the crowd and appears to be following you. You try to get a peek of his face over your shoulder but he is wearing a heavy cloak with a hood. You notice the glint of a sword at his belt and decide to keep walking... fast.

After a few minutes it looks like you've lost him and now you can hear a roaring commotion in the next field. You investigate further and see a sight that you've never seen before. The bear baiting!

Turn to page 30.

After breakfast you find yourself waiting up a tree with the same four men you first met. You are going to ambush the next rich traveller who passes beneath.

You are all watching a young girl approach. She is pretty and has two guards with her. The guards carry heavy-looking packages on their horses. "This should be easy," whispers the small rat-faced leader.

Just then you hear a tinkling of bells and a coloured wagon comes rattling down the road going in the opposite direction. '*Barber Surgeon and Respected Physician',* read blue letters painted on the side of the wagon.

If you wait for the wagon to pass and rob the pretty girl when it is out of sight, turn to page 87.

If you decide that the wagon must contain something worth stealing and rob it instead, turn to page 108.

A few hours later, through a gap in the trees, you notice the town that you saw when you first arrived. Even the trees seem familiar. You must be walking in circles!

You grit your teeth thinking about the physician. The 'cure-all' medicine hasn't made any difference. Now you feel worse than ever.

A bird of prey screeches overhead as you climb a gentle hill, the smell of earth and nature all around you. Then, through the trees in front of you, you catch a glimpse of a sudden bright blue flash.

Dashing towards the light you come across the biggest surprise ever!

Turn to page 126.

Your eyes flicker open but all you see is a bright white blur.

Could it be that you are back in the present?

A minute later you try your eyes again. This time the white is more focused and you can make out a shape on the wall in front of you: a large wooden crucifix. The room you are in is tiny and painted entirely white and you realise you are lying on a hard bed. You see your clothes neatly folded on a nearby chair. Someone speaks.

"Welcome back."

You turn your head and see before you a man dressed in a rough brown robe with another crucifix around his neck. His hair is cut to reveal a small bald patch on the centre of his head although he is young. This man is a monk.

"We thought we had lost you for a while," he continues. "You've taken a nasty blow to the head my child."

You put a hand to your head and feel blood matted into your hair. *How long have you been unconscious?*

Turn to page 13.

You peep through the straw again and see that you are passing through a courtyard, ringing with the shouts of young squires and the calls of animals. The cart comes to an abrupt stop directly under the walls of the central keep – a thick-walled, square tower at the centre of the castle complex. The driver gets down from the cart and disappears off around the corner.

Now's your chance!

You slip out from under the straw and look around for somewhere to run to. The only option seems to be a small window above the cart. Using the cart as a platform, you climb through the window and at once your nostrils are assailed by the smells of a fine banquet.

You creep along the narrow stone passages of the inner castle towards the smell and come to a thick red curtain. There seems to be a medieval banquet taking place today. You wonder if Sir Donald is already here, then boldly push the curtain aside and step out into the great hall.

Turn to page 6.

116

While you gobble down the pottage, which as it happens isn't so bad when you're starving, Sir Donald pops outside calling that he'll be back in a moment. You gather your things and stand in the doorway shivering in the chilly morning breeze. *Where did he go?*

A moment later your question is answered by the clip-clop of a horse. Sir Donald rides around the corner looking magnificent, sat on the back of an enormous warhorse. In that chain mail with the multi-coloured over-garments and a broadsword at his hip, he certainly does look a picture!

"Come valiant one. Ride with me." Sir Donald grins and gestures for you to jump up behind him. Feeling like royalty you trot off happily into the countryside.

Turn to page 75.

You turn back to the girl and lift her into your arms. She barely weighs more than a skeleton. "How did you end up here Matilda?" you ask.

"My parents brought me out here and left me," she begins to sob, coughing and choking. You look at her dirty blanket and notice spots of blood all over it.

"Are you hurt?" You begin to check her arms and legs for wounds.

"I feel bad," she moans, "really bad." You don't find any wounds on her body but you do discover curious black growths under her arms. They look like they're about to burst.

With a surprised grunt she throws up all over you and falls to the ground silent.

You wipe the vomit from your face with her blanket. Now you understand what Sir Donald was trying to tell you. The Plague! The Pestilence! This little innocent girl was more dangerous than a hundred outlaws and now you are going to find out what it is to suffer the torments of the Black Death.

The End

118

You've had quite enough ale for one afternoon so you decide to have a stroll and see what's happening at the fair. You pay Barnaby the innkeeper with the few pennies that you have and he is more than pleased. Barnaby, sweating and grinning like a Cheshire cat, shakes your hand again and bids you farewell.

You leave the gloom and smoky atmosphere of the inn and step out into bright sunshine which blinds you for a few moments. When your eyes have adjusted you can see the vibrant colours of the medieval fair in the distance.

Turn to page 111.

You get dressed quietly. A reverberating snore from the fireside chair tells you that Sir Donald is still fast asleep. You slip out of the window glancing back to memorise Sir Donald's house number in case you need to return in the dark. Number sixty-six, an easy number to remember.

The strange dancing light is more distant now, getting closer to the edge of the forest. You jog towards the light but stop short when you realise that the light is accompanied by voices. It sounds like a small group of men. Gruff voices whisper to each other. As you creep closer you see that the dancing light is merely a torch held by one of the men. In the darkness of the night you can't make out their faces but they appear to be searching for something, or someone. Maybe they could help you find the time machine? A wolf howls in the distance startling you and instinctively you crouch low using the shadows to hide yourself from sight.

If you want to creep back to the warm bed at Sir Donald's house before he notices you are gone, turn to page 85.

If you think these men could help you on your quest and decide to bravely leave the cover of the shadows, turn to page 34.

After an hour you reach an encampment deep in the trees. Sitting by the side of a roaring campfire is the most evil-looking man you have ever seen. He is completely bald with big black eyebrows and piercing blue eyes. A cruel smile plays across his lips. You know immediately that this is Henry.

"Who are you?" he stands and steps towards you menacingly. "You are not from these parts. You look... unfamiliar, strange." He peers into your eyes. *Can he guess where you're really from?* You begin to sweat. It feels like he is looking into your soul. "Sing us a song from *your* village. Entertain us." He sits back down expectantly.

If you start singing and dancing an improvised medieval tune, turn to page 79.

If you have had enough of this man's rudeness and tell him to shut his mouth, turn to page 50.

You really are feeling awful now. You notice a burning pain coming from under your arms. Lifting your shirt you see a bulbous black growth under each armpit. *Why is this familiar?* Of course, the old woman had the same growths on her neck!

Then the most horrifying thought enters your head – your school history class. You remember doing a medieval project about the plague. You also remember the symptoms: coughing, headache, a rancid smell and black 'buboes' appearing under the arms, in the groin and on the neck! *But how?*

It hits you then, like a shock in a nightmare... the old woman. You kissed her!

You collapse into the worst fit of coughing yet and fall to the ground. You wipe your mouth and notice fresh blood glistening on the back of your hand.

Although you try, you never get up from that spot again.

The End

"You are now a prisoner of King Henry and will be taken to him," you say. "Come on men, we'll split the gold later." The men immediately start walking. *Wow! The men are obeying you now. They must see you as their new leader!*

As you trek back under the boughs of the dark forest the princess refuses to speak, only cursing you and muttering insults about Henry. Up above, the leaves sound like human voices whispering to each other as gusts of wind blow through them.

You start to daydream about how you will spend your new-found wealth. Of course you will have to give a large portion to Henry, being your king, but your portion is sure to be enough to buy yourself a horse at least. Maybe even a sword! You've always wanted to own a real medieval sword.

Your daydreaming is interrupted by a rhythmic thumping sound, at first distant but drawing nearer and nearer with each passing second.

Turn to page 36.

The man leads you, flitting from door to door, through a network of narrow alleyways.

Eventually you arrive at a small wattle and daub house and the man directs you inside.

You feel anxious but as the candles are lit and the shutters opened you see that it's really quite a cosy looking place. There is a small fire crackling in the corner and you breathe in the smell of leather and incense.

Passing you a steaming mug of mulled wine, the man at last introduces himself as 'Sir Donald of Pudleigh', a chivalrous knight of the realm.

Turn to page 80.

Your belly swells as you eat more than you've ever eaten before. Sweetmeats, roasted birds of all types, delicious puddings all washed down with wine and mead.

Feeling full and sleepy you accidentally push down on the return device in your pocket. At the same moment a turquoise-blue flash catches your eye. It is coming from the massive fireplace. Nobody else seems to have noticed. A blue flash can only mean one thing... the time machine; your only ticket home.

It must have re-located to the castle when it disappeared and by luck you have activated it.

Now is your only chance!

You jump up from the table and make a dash for the fireplace.

"Where are you going?" calls Sir Donald, spilling his wine in surprise.

"Far, far away," you call back. "Goodbye and thank you for everything." You reach the fireplace and jump into the source of the blue light, pressing down on the button of the return device.

Sir Donald and the king look at each other slack-jawed and the whole room gasps at the explosion of blue flashes. After a few seconds of total silence, amazed whispers begin to echo from the stone walls.

Turn to page 48.

The shutters creak open as you slide your arm inside looking for a handhold so you can pull yourself up. You are just starting to struggle up and in through the window when a sudden, searing pain tears through your arm and you find yourself falling back down onto the grass.

"What have I done!" moans Sir Donald staring down at you from between the shutters. "I thought you were… you were… oh woe is me."

You notice the sword in his hand dripping with blood, *your blood!* "I'm so sorry. When I saw your empty bed I thought you had been taken, I thought *they* were here," splutters Sir Donald.

You follow Sir Donald's horrified gaze to your right side but there is nothing there. Your right arm has been completely cut off! Now the pain hits you.

Before you lose consciousness you feel Sir Donald lifting you in his arms and muttering something about a local healer. Your knowledge of medieval medicine doesn't fill you with confidence and you are not sure how long you will last.

The End

You run towards the blue flash, push a few branches to the side and stare through into a small clearing... at yourself!

What?

You rub your eyes hard and stare again.

You are looking at yourself standing next to the time machine. The blue flash must have been the machine arriving. That's when you realise you're looking at exactly the same spot where you first arrived. Somehow you are seeing yourself in the moment when you first stepped out of the time machine. There must be a glitch in the space time continuum!

It dawns on you then that you are looking at your only means of escape.

As soon as the 'second you' steps away from the machine and turns their back, you make a run for it.

You sprint across the clearing being careful not to make a sound. Then, pressing the button down on your return device, you leap into the empty machine. With another blue flash you are gone.

Turn to page 44.

After a while the gentle rocking of the cart soothes you off to sleep, but some hours later you are jolted awake by the sudden scraping of iron chains. The sun, high in the sky, tells you that morning has long since arrived.

Looking out from under the straw you see the massive stone walls of the castle directly in front of you. The drawbridge has just been lowered.

You think fast. If you stay hidden, maybe the cart will take you into the castle but if you are caught hiding you will surely be executed as a spy.

You are not even sure if you want to get into this castle. Shouldn't you be searching for the time machine after all?

If you risk staying hidden and wait to see where you'll end up, turn to page 74.

If you think it's safer to get out of the cart and slip away before you enter the castle, turn to page 93.

Roast boar and wine? You're not one to turn down food so you trot after the four men, leaving the cramped streets of the town and following a path out into the surrounding forest.

During the trek you learn that these men are in fact soldiers. Your instincts were correct. They fight for a great lord called Henry who is the rightful king of the land. They tell you of Edward, Henry's bitter enemy, who also claims to be king but is a soft and weak leader.

"We will cut him down like wheat," yells one of the men swinging his sword at an invisible foe. "A king should be strong and ruthless and our Henry is certainly that," he grins.

Turn to page 120.

21528163R00080

Printed in Poland
by Amazon Fulfillment
Poland Sp. z o.o., Wrocław